AESOP'S
AWESOME
RHYMES

THE TOWN MOUSE
AN' THE COUNTRY MOUSE

To Matey and Mogs
L.K.

With love to Maya Town Mouse,
from your friend, Country Mouse
J.N.

ORCHARD BOOKS
338 Euston Road, London NW1 3BH
Orchard Books Australia
Level 17/207 Kent Street, Sydney, NSW 2000

First published in 2011
First paperback publication in 2012

ISBN 978 1 40830 962 9 (hardback)
ISBN 978 1 40830 970 4 (paperback)

Text © Lou Kuenzler 2011
Illustrations © Jill Newton 2011

The rights of Lou Kuenzler to be identified as the author and
Jill Newton to be identified as the illustrator of this work
has been asserted by them in accordance
with the Copyright, Designs and Patents Act, 1988.

A CIP catalogue record for this book is available
from the British Library.

1 3 5 7 9 10 8 6 4 2 (hardback)
1 3 5 7 9 10 8 6 4 2 (paperback)

Printed in Great Britain

Orchard Books is a division of Hachette Children's Books,
an Hachette UK company.
www.hachette.co.uk

THE TOWN MOUSE
AND THE COUNTRY MOUSE

Written by **Lou Kuenzler**
Illustrated by **Jill Newton**

ORCHARD

Old Aesop was an Ancient Greek –
his AWESOME FABLES are unique.
Each fun tale gives good advice
reminding us we must be nice.

Do not be spoilt, don't scream and shout.
Try not to moan or sulk or pout.
Don't pull your sister by the hair
or feed your brother to a bear.
Please listen to this good advice
and heed my tale of foolish mice!

In this cool fable you can read
about the things we really need . . .

It all begins with a tiny mouse –
her quiet life and country house.
Mousy lived on nuts and seeds
and strolled among the grass and reeds.

Until, one late October day . . .
her cousin, Grey Mouse, came to stay.

Cousin Grey had come from town:
"It's cool to meet you, Mousy Brown!"
Mousy showed him round her home –
a sandy hole beneath a stone.

"Gee!" said Grey. "It's really small!
There's hardly any room at all."

Grey's whiskers twitched. He didn't think
that he could stand the country stink!
There was an awful *dung-heap* smell —
which perfume shops would NEVER sell.

Brown showed him where she liked to sit.

I use this log to rest and knit.
I gather wool from grazing sheep,
so careful where you put your feet!

She spoke too late! Grey's trendy shoe
went *splat!* into a pile of poo.
"Man! Oh, man! That sheep poo smells!
My shoes are RUINED!" Grey Mouse
 yelled.

"I'm sorry, Grey," said Mousy Brown.
"I guess you don't get sheep in town!
Go down to the stream to wash –
I'll fix us both some country nosh!"

As he washed, Grey's mood improved –
he liked the thought of wholesome food.

"Lunch is ready," Mousy cried.
She brought a bowl of seeds outside.
Grey could not believe his eyes.
"But where are all the cakes and pies?"

Mousy blushed. "This is your lot.
I've shared the only food I've got.
The autumn fruits are nearly gone.
Winter will come before too long."

"You mean I'll soon get stuck in snow?"
Grey leapt up. "I've got to go!
I cannot STAND this quiet place.
I need more food to STUFF MY FACE!
I'm sorry if I've let you down,
but I am heading BACK TO TOWN!"

But then Grey had a good idea . . .
Why should Mousy stay round here?

Don't fester in this dump alone,
when you could visit me at home.
Come down to town, my country cuz!
And then you'll have a real buzz!

Mousy shivered. "You think I should?
I've never been beyond that wood!"
"So take a risk and come," said Grey.
"It's time you had a trip away!"

"Ok," said Mousy. "Yes – I 'll come!"
Grey grinned. "I'll show you so much fun!"

Dragging Mousy by her paw,
Grey took her on a whirlwind tour.
Busy shops took Mousy's breath.

A show called *Cats* scared her to death!

Next the Museum of Modern Art . . .
Poor Mousy felt she'd fall apart.

"I've seen so much, my mind's a blur!
I've smoky whiskers, dusty fur.
My legs are tired, my feet are sore.
I just can't lift another paw!"

"OK!" Grey nodded. "Home to eat!
And you can rest your tired feet."
Once inside Grey's city home,
Mousy forgot her aching bones.
She could only stand and stare.
Food was piled EVERYWHERE!

"Perfect timing!" smiled Grey Mouse.

There's a party in the house.
While they're drinking in the lounge,
let's climb the table, feast and scrounge!

Mousy's eyes grew big as saucers —
soon her mouth began to water.
She saw croissants, butter, jam,

salami, burgers, chicken, ham,

lemonade, cola, ginger ale,
milkshakes, smoothies, ice in a pail.

Apples, pears, grapes and melons,
mango, cherries, limes and lemons.

Pink iced buns, cinnamon swirls,
cupcakes, brownies, Viennese whirls,

trifle, ice cream, crumble, jelly.
Tasty things that fill your belly!

Best of all for Mousy – cheese!
"Look! There's tons of kinds of these!
Edam, Cheddar, Camembert too.
Parmesan, Gouda, Shropshire Blue.

Mozzarella, Brie, and feta –
Mouse food doesn't get much better!"

"It's like a dream!" cried Mousy Brown.
"I think I'll come and live in town!"

"Cool!" said Grey. "Now, let's tuck in!"
But suddenly a man came in.
He'd come for cake, or something nice.
He didn't see the startled mice.

Grey dived down, flat on his belly.
Mousy hid behind a jelly.
Shaking like the big dessert,
her heart was pounding till it hurt.

Her shivers wobbled all the spoons
and jiggled bunches of balloons.
The man cried, "Goodness! Something
   shook.
I'd better go and take a look."

Mousy quivered: "It's the end!"
But heard a call from the man's friend:
"Bring some cakes," he yelled downstairs.
The man cried, "Right!" and grabbed
  eclairs.

"Lucky escape!" whistled Grey Mouse.
"There's danger in a party house."
"I'm *so* afraid!" cried Mousy Brown.
"It's much too scary here in town!"

"Chill out!" said Grey. "It's no big deal.
Let's just enjoy this AWESOME meal!"

So Mousy promised she'd relax.
She helped herself to cheesy snacks.
A little Brie and Danish Blue.
But suddenly a cat walked through!

In one swift bound the tabby beast
had pounced amid the party feast.
Grey dived into a bowl of mash –
and vanished with a soggy splash.

Mousy hid behind a plum . . .
Too late! The cat had seen her run.
"Purrrrfect!" purred Puss. "A quick
   mouse treat!
I wanted something small to eat!"

"Leave me alone!" poor Mousy cried,
and jumped on a banana slide.

...down she slid ...
saw a hole in the wall and hid.

The tabby puss prowled round and round.
Mousy tried to make no sound.
But this was SCARY hide and seek,
and Mousy could not help but squeak:

**Oh save me please! Do something, Grey!
Make this TIGER go away!**

"Cool down!" hissed Grey. "Don't have
   a fit.
We'll easily fool this big old kit!"

But Tabby followed Mousy's call
and peered inside the broken wall.

He flicked a spiky, pointed claw,
and dragged her out across the floor.

"Yum," he purred and arched his back,
"it's time I had a little snack!"
Quicker than a lightning flash,
Grey leapt from the bowl of mash.
He shook potato from his hair
and chucked a sausage through the air.

"Hey, Tabby Puss! Yo, Kitty Cat!
Here's a sausage. Just try that."
While greedy Tabby sniffed the meat
Mousy jumped quickly to her feet.
She ran behind a big, old clock
quivering from her dreadful shock.

Luckily Tabby was lazy and fat –
"A sausage!" he said. "I'll settle for that."
And with the treat between his jaws,
he padded off to eat next door.

"It's safe now, Cuz. Come out," said Grey.
"I've fed the beast. He's gone away!"

Then – BONG! – they heard the
tall clock strike –
a sound poor Mousy didn't like.

"I just can't take this any more!"
she cried and ran across the floor.

In town I live just like a queen –
but this is the scariest place I've been.
I've never seen such awesome feasts,
but I just want to live in peace.

44

"Don't go home!" begged Cousin Grey.
"You'd soon like town, if you'd just stay!"
Mousy hated being unkind.
Should she stay and change her mind?
But, suddenly, a guard dog pup
charged inside to gobble them up.

"Goodbye!" cried Mousy, turning to flee.
"This hectic life is not for me.
Everything here is far too manic –
I'm always in a dreadful panic."

She missed quiet meadows, hedges,
  trees . . .
the stink of sheep poo on the breeze!

Although my little house is poor,
I love it! I want nothing more!

Aesop's moral now seems clear:
Better poor in peace than rich in fear!

AESOP'S AWESOME RHYMES

Written by Lou Kuenzler
Illustrated by Jill Newton

All priced at £4.99

Orchard Books are available
from all good bookshops, or can
be ordered from our website,
www.orchardbooks.co.uk,
or telephone 01235 827702,
or fax 01235 827703.